"People all know their birthdays,
the day they were born.
But the day they will die is something
no person knows.

The only one who knows,
the one who decides the day
is me, the Reaper."

"I, the Reaper, take any form
I wish.
Flower, grass or tree
I can be,
even cloud or sky."

"Ah yes,
you see that piglet
by my side.
The poor thing will be dying
in a few days."
Near the Reaper
lay a piglet in pain.
At that moment—

A hungry wolf
came by.
"W–W–Was someone
speaking just now?"
The wolf looked
hither, thither and around.
"I–I guess not.
W–What a creepy
forest this is,"
the wolf said,
body trembling.

"Oh, I'm hungry...
I'd love something
good to eat.
But there's no way
any delicious piglet
would be here,"
the wolf spoke
and spun—

F-FOUND YOU—

"Cute piglet,
you look delicious!"
The wolf
leaped forth
to gobble down the piglet.
But—

"Phew…"
the piglet breathed
painfully.

"T-This one is sick…
It looks good to eat but is sick.
Right! I'll wait until it gets better
then eat it! Heheh,"
the wolf said
and went home carrying the piglet.

"Ah yes, that wolf too
will be dying
in a few days.
Why, it's just
a cunning, disliked wolf.
It can't be helped.
                Ho ho ho!"

Back home,
the wolf tucked in the piglet
on the wolf's own bed,
nice and soft.

Gulping down saliva the wolf said,
"Yummy…
Now get well soon. When you do,
I'll eat you! Heheh…"
Meanwhile, the wolf itself

chose the hard floor
and slept without a blanket.

The Reaper
silently gazed at the two.

The morning after,
the wolf sang,
"Oink, Oink, Oinky~♪"
for the piglet and danced,
twisting its body, wriggling its butt
to the silly ditty.
"How's that? Isn't it fun? Recover soon
so we can sing and dance together."

"It won't recover.
In fact, you two
will soon die,"
the Reaper said
and shut his eyes.

The wolf visited a meadow
the next day too.
Picking flowers,
it suddenly remembered.

"I know!
My grandpa once told me of a plant
with red petals and leaves
that can cure
any ill if you eat it!
Right!"

Since that day the wolf
set out day after day looking
for the red plant.
On rainy days,

on windy days,
no matter how tired,
it went looking.
But the all-red plant was
nowhere to be found.

"W-Why are you giving up,
and not trying to get better?
Why aren't you trying to live?
Once you recover, there will be
fun things, nice things, many things!
Didn't you want me to eat you?
Then get well! Do you understand me?"

"Y-Y-Yes,"
said the piglet,
shut its eyes
and slept.

The next day,
searching for the red plant,
the wolf came to a cliff
past the forest.

"Whoa! I-I-I must
take care not to fall off."
Just as the wolf said this
and peeked down the cliff,
"Ohh!"
it saw a red plant
swaying in the wind.

"Yes! I finally found it!"
the wolf said full of glee,

while the Reaper said
full of sorrow,
"It's just that none who
go down this cliff
make it back alive..."

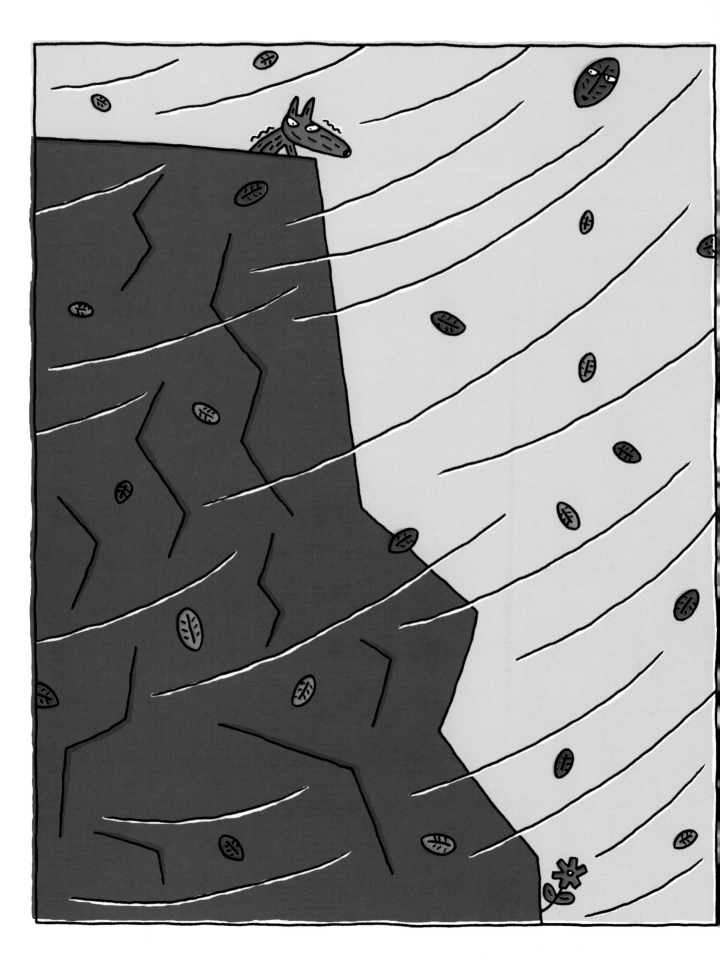

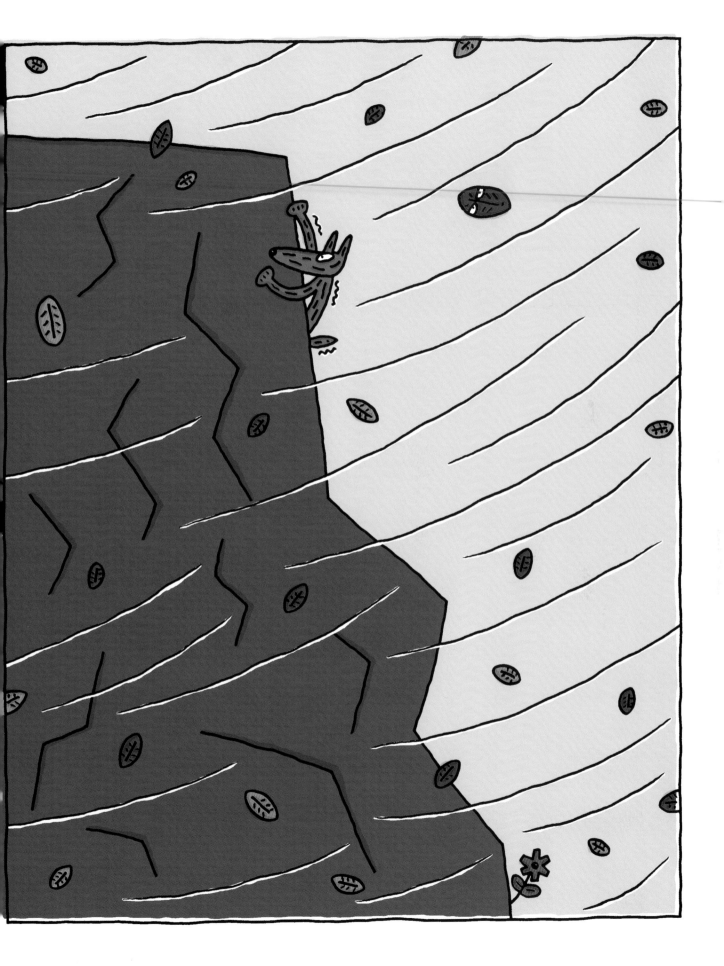

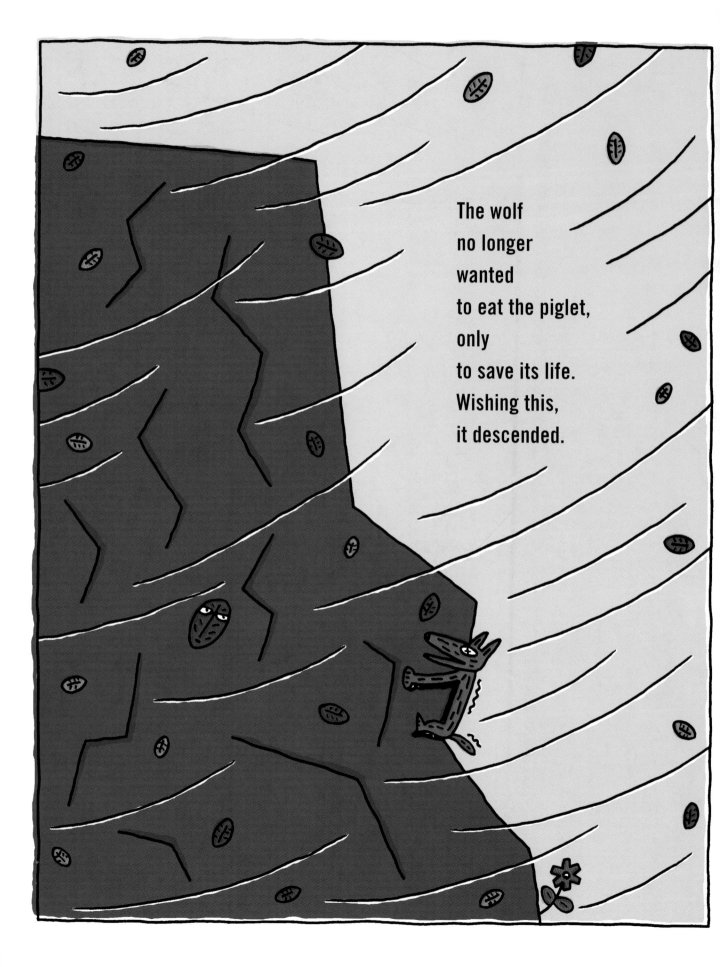

"A-A-Almost…"
The wolf reached
its paw out.

When it gripped
a leaf—

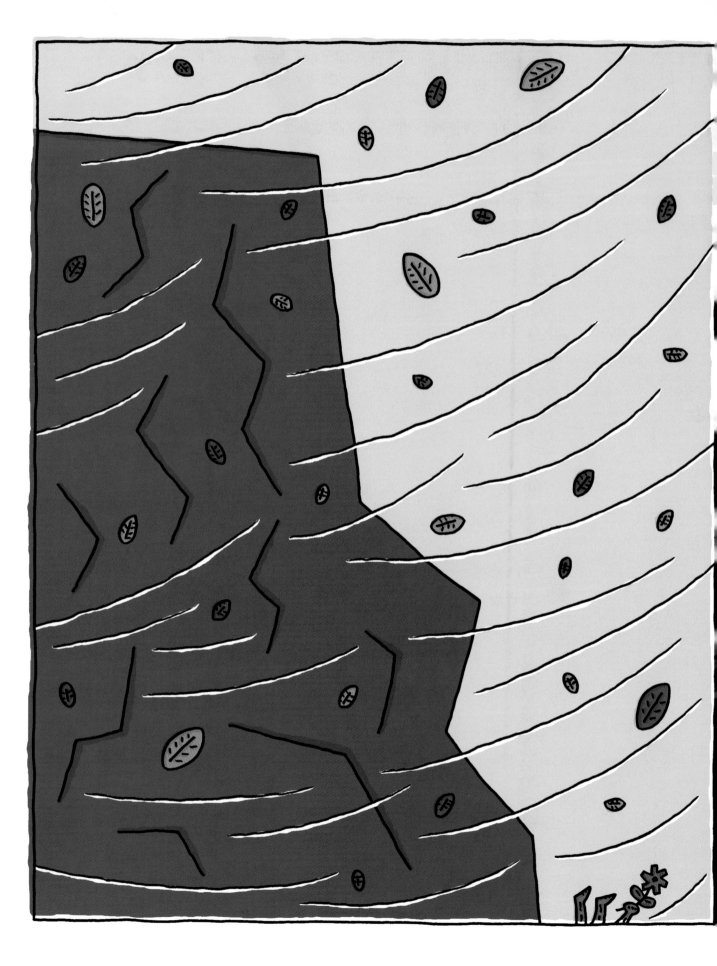

A few days passed.
"Ho ho ho... Just like I said,
that wolf fell off a cliff,
and the piglet didn't get cured and died.
...Do you think?
What do you believe?

At the moment, the two—

"dance in a meadow.
Bodies twisting, butts wriggling
to that silly ditty they're happily singing."

TWIST

WRIGGLE

"Oink ♪ Oink ♪
Oinky~
Well and Good
Oinky Oink ♪

Oi-Oi ♪ Oi-Oi ♪
Oi~ Oi~
Twist Wriggle
Oi~ Oi~ ♪"

"Y-You ask me how they're alive?
Well, I didn't want to see such
a wonderful pair die, not me. Ho ho ho..."

About the Author

Born in 1956, Tatsuya Miyanishi is currently one of the
most popular children's book authors in Japan. A graduate
of the Nihon University College of Art, he began his career
as a graphic designer and has worked on paper dramas,
planetarium programming, and textbook illustrations
in addition to the picture books that have won him the
Kodansha Publishing Culture Award. While his works have
been translated into French, Chinese, and Korean in the
past, *Mr. Reaper* marks his English-language debut.

Mr. Reaper
Story and art by Tatsuya Miyanishi

Story and art © 2010 by Tatsuya Miyanishi
Translation © 2012 by Vertical, Inc.

Published by Vertical, Inc., New York

Originally published in Japanese as *Shinigami-san*
by Ehon No Mori, Tokyo, 2010.

ISBN 978-1-935654-28-5

Manufactured in Malaysia

First Edition

Vertical, Inc.
451 Park Avenue South, 7th Floor
New York, NY 10016
www.vertical-inc.com